Dora Bruder

by Patrick Modiano

BOOK ANALYSIS

Written by Yolanda Fernández Romero
Translated by Oliver Brown

Dora Bruder

BY PATRICK MODIANO

PATRICK MODIANO

FRENCH WRITER, SCRIPTWRITER, ESSAYIST AND LYRICIST

- **Born in 1945 in Boulogne-Billancourt (Hauts-de-Seine)**

- **Some of his works:**

  - *Les Boulevards de Ceinture* (1972), novel

  - *Rue des Boutiques Obscures* (1978), novel

  - *So That You Don't Get Lost In the Neighbourhood* (2014), novel

Patrick Modiano was born to a Flemish actress mother and a Jewish father from Alexandria (Egypt). His works always have an autobiographical aspect and regularly feature his father. After running away from home on numerous occasions in his adolescence, he was introduced to the literary world by Raymond Queneau (French writer, 1903-1976), who helped him publish his first book, *La Place de l'Étoile*, in 1968.

Patrick Modiano won the Nobel Prize for Literature in 2014 and has also received several awards during his career, including the Grand Prix du roman de l'Académie française for *Les Boulevards de Ceinture* and the Goncourt Prize for *Rue des Boutiques Obscures*. His novels are set mainly in Paris during the Occupation (1940-1944) and focus on the lives of ordinary people, as Modiano dutifully brings to life the experiences of those who lived through that period.

DORA BRUDER

A FICTIONAL INVESTIGATION

- **Genre:** novel (autofiction)

- **Reference edition:** *Dora Bruder*, Paris, Gallimard, "Folio" collection, 2015, 160 p.

- **1st edition:** 1997

- **Themes :** biography, investigation, duty to remember, Occupation, deportation

Published in 1997, *Dora Bruder* is the story of an investigation led by Patrick Modiano to retrace the life of Dora Bruder (1926-1942), who disappeared at the age of 15. Following the discovery of a wanted poster in *Paris-Soir*, dating from 1941, the author becomes obsessed with bringing Dora's life to light. He tries to reconstruct the life of this young Jewish girl from Paris, with whom he identifies.

Dora Bruder takes up the themes dear to Modiano: the period of the Occupation, the situation of Jews in Paris, autobiographical elements, and the work of memory. Extracting ordinary individuals from anonymity, *Dora Bruder* is also a meeting point for many lives that intersect, intermingle, or live in parallel.

A WANTED NOTICE

In 1988, Patrick Modiano discovered an old newspaper dated 31 December 1941 containing a wanted notice issued by parents terrified by the disappearance of their 15-year-old daughter, Dora Bruder: "We are looking for a young girl, Dora Bruder, 15 years old, 1.55 m, oval face, grey-brown eyes, grey sports coat, burgundy jumper, navy blue skirt and hat, brown sports shoes. Send all indications to M. and Mme.Bruder, 41 boulevard Ornano, Paris." (p. 7).

Obsessed by the image and story of this young girl, Modiano patiently investigates for more than ten years: "I am patient, I can wait for hours in the rain," (p.14) he confides. He endeavours to reconstruct the life of Dora, a young Jewish woman living in Paris under the German occupation, detained by the French police after running away and deported to Auschwitz. He discovers information little by little: the wanted notice, her place of residence, her date and place of birth, the school she attended, etc.

Having also run away from home at the same age, the author recognises himself in this young girl and wishes to bring her out of anonymity. To do this, he consults official documents and police records, conducts interviews, and follows up every lead like a real detective. He also manages to find a cousin of Dora's, who provides him with some information, but above all with family photos, which add to the elements he has already gathered.

PARIS UNDER THE OCCUPATION

Modiano shares with the reader his research, his doubts, and his findings, which he delivers in the form of a precise and methodical police report. For Modiano, this investigation is a great opportunity to depict the Paris of the Occupation, to recall the norms and rules that Jews had to respect at the time, to talk about detention centres and roundups and, finally, to find the traces of missing and forgotten people. In this frantic collection of information, he found documents on Dora's father, Ernest Bruder – born in Vienna, but stateless – and on her mother, Cécile Bruder – born in Budapest, a Jew of Russian origin – both of whom died in Auschwitz, as did their daughter.

Dora, a young girl placed in a Catholic boarding school – a "boarding school for five hundred workers' daughters, with seventy-five sisters" (p. 39) – at the Saint-Cœur-de-Marie, rue de Picpus, runs away twice. In the first case, her father waited 13 days before reporting her disappearance. He was probably slow to do so because he had not declared his daughter's existence during the compulsory census of Jews in October 1940. Rather than protecting her, he risked putting her in danger. On 17 April 1942, Dora was returned to her mother, while her father was already interned in the Drancy camp (Île-de-France).

She ran away a second time. To find her, her mother decided to call on the UGIF (Union Générale des Israélites de France). The police report emphasised that because of her successive runaways, it would be appropriate to place her in a reformatory for children. In addition, the report mentions her mother's state of indigence, as well as her father's confinement. On 19 June 1942, Dora was interned at the Tourelles barracks, under the number 439, with five other girls her age. A few days later, the first convoy of women left the barracks and France.

Cécile, Dora's mother, was arrested on 16 July 1942 during a major round-up. She was reunited with her husband at Drancy. A few days later, she was released.

On 13 August of the same year, Dora was transferred to Drancy, where she was also reunited with her father. At the beginning of September, she had the possibility of being transferred to the Pithiviers camp (Loiret), which is only possible for Jews of French nationality. But Dora preferred to stay in Drancy, near her father. Both were sent to the Auschwitz extermination camp on 18 September, along with 1,000 other men and women.

Cécile was interned again in the Drancy camp on 9 January 1943. A month later, five months after her husband and daughter, she was sent to Auschwitz. None of them would return.

THE AUTOBIOGRAPHICAL SCOPE

Depicting the life of Dora Bruder is also an opportunity for Modiano to talk about himself. In fact, he draws many parallels between his life and that of the young girl: he mentions his childhood, his familiarity with the Boulevard Ornano neighbourhood, his mother, his twentieth birthday celebrated in Vienna, his taste for wandering around the city, his readings (such as *Les Misérables* [novel by Victor Hugo (1802-1885), 1862] and *Miracle de la rose* [novel by Jean Genet (1910-1986), 1946]), and his elopement on 18 January 1960.

He also talks about his father, Albert Modiano, and the distant relationship he has with him. Revealing some of his secrets, he tells us that one day his father reported him to the police for having asked him to pay the monthly pension he owed to his mother: a "ruffian," he tells them, "was making a scandal" (p. 69) in his home.

In *Dora Bruder*, the author feels the need to free himself from this Jewish father who lived in Paris illegally during the Occupation, earned his living on the black market and separated from his wife and son: a father with whom he never got along and whom he stopped seeing in his late teens. He tried to see his father one last time, 20 years later, but after wandering in vain in the hospital where he was placed, he could not find him and turned back. He never saw him again.

At the end of the novel, the author, having reached the end of his investigation, notes that Dora, her personality, her emotions, and the reasons for her running away remain a mystery that the narrator has only been able to approach through his imagination and suppositions: 'This is her secret [...], which [her] executioners [...] could not have stolen from her.' (p. 69).

CHARACTER STUDY

THE BRUDERS

Dora Bruder

Dora Bruder is the character around whom the novel is organized: she is the object of the narrator's investigation and gives the story its title. She is a young Jewish girl, French, "15 years old, 5'5", oval face, grey-brown eyes" (p. 42); "Very young, according to her cousin, she was already rebellious, independent, a runaway" (p. 34).

Thus, at the age of 14, Dora is placed in the Saint-Cœur-de-Marie boarding school: "Her parents felt that she needed discipline" (p. 38). However, she does not want to submit to the rules of the boarding school and runs away. Not content with escaping once, she runs away a second time and ends up in the Tourelles camp. These escapades, the reasons for which are not really known, nevertheless underline her determination and her independent character.

Although Modiano manages to reconstruct the facts in broad outline, little is known about her character, her relationship with her parents and her social life: "I don't know whether Dora Bruder made friends at the Saint-Cœur-de-Marie. Or whether she remained aloof from the others." (p. 42). After her internment at Les Tourelles, she was deported to the Drancy camp and was part of convoy no. 34 on 18 September 1942, bound for Auschwitz, where she died.

This character, whose life the author seeks to reconstruct, becomes a double of Modiano, an alter ego with whom he identifies, forced to fill in the gaps in his investigation with his own interpretations, which are in large part personal projections. Moreover, this anonymous young girl, one of many victims of the Second World War (1939-1945), becomes an icon in Modiano's writing; she embodies youth under the Occupation, but also an emblematic figure of the victims of the Shoah (the extermination of some 6,000,000 Jews by the Nazis during the Second World War).

Ernest Bruder

Ernest Bruder, Dora's father, was born on 21 May 1899 in Vienna and works as a factory worker. His niece, interviewed by the author, recalls "[h]is kindness and gentleness" (p. 28). Ernest found himself in Paris at the age of 25, released from his enlistment in the French Foreign Legion as a private, probably as a result of an injury. A police form, drawn up in the context of the roundups organised during the Occupation, mentions his status as a "100% war cripple". Despite his commitment, he did not obtain French nationality, and was therefore considered stateless by the French state. It was in Paris that he met the woman who would become Dora's mother.

When the Second World War broke out, Ernest Bruder no longer worked; he lived with his wife and daughter in a hotel room. When the time came to report himself as a Jew to the local police station, he did not mention the existence of his daughter, to protect her. Arrested on 19 March

1942, he was interned in Drancy. He was later deported to the Auschwitz camp, from where he never returned.

Cécile Bruder

Born in Budapest on April 17, 1907, to a Jewish family of Russian origin, Cécile Bruder married Ernest Bruder in 1924, when she was only 16 years old. A seamstress, Cécile had been living in Paris for a year with her parents, her brother and her four sisters, who died of typhoid fever as soon as they arrived.

During the war, when Ernest was deported, police reports indicate that she was living in great poverty. After her daughter ran away, she called on the Union Générale des Israélites de France, in desperation.

She was interned at Drancy during the great roundup of 16 July 1942. She was reunited with Ernest for a few days, before being released on 23 July. She was locked up again in the same place on 9 January 1943, then transferred to Auschwitz in February, where she died like her husband and daughter.

THE MODIANOS

Albert Modiano

Patrick Modiano's father is an omnipresent figure in his works. In *Dora Bruder*, the author evokes a father of Jewish origin, with whom he does not get along very well; a father who chooses to live underground and to participate in the black market in order to survive during the Occupation. Nevertheless, the author makes no judgement on this choice: "It was legitimate for them to behave like outlaws in order to survive. That is their honour. And I love them for it." (p. 117). However, living under a false identity does not save him from arrest; Albert Modiano is indeed apprehended during a raid, but manages to escape.

In the course of the investigation, parallels are drawn between the life of the young Dora and that of Albert Modiano. The author takes the opportunity to write of disputes and intimate moments with her father. Albert Modiano appears as a distant person, not very talkative, who does not share much with his son. Cold and inflexible, he goes so far as to denounce him to the police for his allegedly "thuggish" behaviour (p. 69): "We were sitting opposite each other on the wooden benches, each surrounded by two peacekeepers." (*ibid.*).

After this scene, father and son only saw each other a few times, before definitively breaking the link: "I was to see him again two or three times the following year [...] He stole my military papers to try to have me forcibly incorporated into the Reuilly barracks [Indre]. After that, I never saw him again." (p. 72).

Patrick Modiano

Author, narrator and character of the novel, Patrick Modiano reveals himself through his investigation of Dora Bruder. A determined and meticulous man, he shows patience and invests himself totally in the mission of bringing the Bruder family back to life. Obsessed by the traces of time, the duty of memory and the absurdity of war, he seeks to revive the memory of the disappeared by piercing the "thick layer of amnesia" (p. 131) deposited on the city by time.

In his fifties when he writes, he evokes his youth and childhood in small steps in the story. The son of divorced parents, born in 1945 to a Jewish father, he is marked by the history of the Shoah.

He spent his childhood with his mother, financially dependent on the meagre pension paid by his father. He recalls outings with his mother to the Saint-Ouen flea market, in the neighbourhood where the Bruder family lived. Abandoned by his father, from whom he is definitively separated at the end of his adolescence (p. 17), he is nevertheless shaped by the story of his arrest during a round-up in 1942, as well as by the clandestine life he had to lead until the end of the war.

Patrick Modiano seems to have always cultivated a free and independent character: at the age of 15, he ran away from home, which he still remembers; a few years later, he chose to stop his studies, then arranged with a doctor to avoid military service; as a young adult, he sold stolen objects to antique dealers. He was an erudite young man with a passion for literature, and wrote *La Place de l'étoile*, his first novel, at the age of 23. In most of the evocations of his youth, he presents himself wandering around Paris, exploring different neighbourhoods, waiting in cafés, soaking up the atmosphere of a city to which he seems inextricably linked.

KEYS TO READING

AN AUTOFICTION?

Dora Bruder is both an autobiographical and biographical story. Jeanne Bem, in an article entitled "*Dora Bruder* ou la biographie déplacée de Modiano" (*Dora Bruder* or Modiano's Displaced Biography), questions the particular genre of the novel, which she describes as "displaced biography, in the sense that nothing is quite in its place" (*Cahiers de l'Association internationale des études françaises*, volume 52, no. 1, 2000, Pp. 221-232). The narrative is indeed built on the principle of autobiography, but also has all the characteristics of biography, while belonging to the fictional text.

A Biographical Novel

With its antecedents in antiquity, in particular in historians such as Plutarch (Greek writer, ca. 50-ca. 125), Tacitus (Latin writer, ca. 55-ca. 120) and Suetonius (Latin writer, ca. 69-ca. 126), the biography is a narrative in which the author tells the life story of a real person.

The biographical genre is thus defined as a "written or oral account, in prose, that a narrator gives of the life of a historical figure, emphasising the singularity of an individual existence and the continuity of a personality" (MADELÉNAT D., *La biographie*, Presses universitaires de France, Paris, 1984, p. 20). The biographer writes in the third person singular. Documented and objective, the account presents the character, the journey, and the evolution of the person.

And *Dora Bruder* is indeed a biographical narrative, since Patrick Modiano assumes the role of biographer of the young Dora, carries out research, produces dated facts and refers to official documents to retrace the young woman's life, as is the case here: "The handrail of the police station in the Clignancourt district bears these indications, dated 27 December 1941." (p. 75)

An Autobiographical Novel

For Philippe Lejeune, autobiography is defined as "the retrospective prose account that a real person gives of his or her own existence, when the focus is on his or her individual life, in particular on the history of his or her personality" (LEJEUNE P., *Le Pacte autobiographique*, Paris, Seuil, 1975, p. 14-15). In fact, an autobiographical novel is a narrative in which the author, the narrator and the main character coincide. The narrative is then written in the first person and from the internal point of view (which leaves a lot of room for subjectivity), since it is the character who tells what he or she has experienced. Moreover, the autobiographical genre implies a very strong reading pact between the reader and the author-narrator, who commits himself to give a sincere account.

The text of *Dora Bruder* is indeed that of an autobio-graphical novel: Patrick Modiano, the narrator of the story, presents himself as the author ("While I write these lines [...]", p. 92) of the story of which he is also a character, since he stages himself in his investigation of Dora Bruder, also evoking distant memories of his childhood or youth ("I sometimes went to the cinema, boulevard Ornano", p. 11). In this way, her personality and her story emerge throughout the text.

A Novel of Autofiction?

Dora Bruder is above all a work of autofiction. Modiano mixes the autobiographical and biographical genres, while giving pride of place to fiction. The concept of 'autofiction', created by Serge Doubrovsky (French critic and novelist, 1928-2017), covers stories with an autobiographical dimension, based on strictly real facts, where an element of fiction enters, linked in particular to the intervention of language, which brings the story into the field of literature. This is the case in *Dora Bruder*, where the account of events is in fact fictionalised, and where the author fills in the gaps in his investigation with his imagination, putting forward hypotheses about the facts or the state of mind of the characters, when his archive work does not allow him to know them.

In this way, Patrick Modiano blurs the codes of biographical and autobiographical narrative by mobilising the narrative forms of fiction and by comparing his own experiences with those of Dora on numerous occasions. He identifies with the young girl, interweaving his own journey with that of the latter. He exhumes her by relying on his own memories to fill in the gaps in the archives and, at the same time, reinvents himself through her:

- the narrator also ran away when he was a teenager, which brings him closer to Dora and enables him to understand her revolt ("I remember the strong impression I felt when I ran away in January 1960 [...]. It was the exhilaration of severing, in one fell swoop, all ties: a brutal and voluntary rupture", p. 77; a "feeling of revolt and solitude brought to its incandescence and which takes your breath away and puts you in weightlessness", p. 78);

- the elopement having given him wings, he thinks that it is this same feeling of freedom that Dora has tasted: "Probably one of the rare occasions in my life when I was really myself and walked at my own pace" (p. 78);

- Ernest Bruder's reference to Vienna, his birthplace, also allows him to talk about his own experience of the capital: "In 1965, I was twenty years old, in Vienna, the same year I was in the Clignancourt district" (p. 21);

- he would like their lives to intersect, through the character of his father, who was also caught in a round-up at the same time as Dora Bruder: "Perhaps I wanted them to intersect, in that winter of 1942" (p. 63);

- long before he became interested in the story of Dora Bruder and the different periods of her life, he himself had wandered around the neighbourhood where she lived in Paris.

Confusion between experience and imagination sets in, and even temporality becomes imprecise. The author, who crosses Dora's life with her own, mixes past and present: "From yesterday to today. As the years go by, the perspectives become blurred for me, the winters blend into each other. The one in 1965 and the one in 1942." (p. 10).

THE SURVEY

The narrative opens with the wanted notice published in *Paris-Soir* on 31 December 1941. This first page sets the framework for what follows; more than a narrative, *Dora Bruder* is a report in simple sentences, which compiles authentic documents and precise descriptions of places. The narrator, like a detective, reveals his systematic and meticulous research method. "Dora Bruder was to be enrolled in one of the local community schools. I wrote a letter to the headmaster of each one," he explains at the beginning of the story (p. 14).

Each lead is followed, and the author shares most of the documents he examines with the reader: birth certificates, Drancy camp files, archives of the Prefecture of Police, Serge Klarsfeld's (French lawyer, born in 1935) *Memorial of the deportation of the Jews of France*, lists of schools in the neighbourhood, archives of communal schools and religious pensions, etc.

Leaving no stone unturned, he also consulted the district court, found a cousin of Dora's as well as some family photos, and wrote to the Sisters of the Catholic school where the girl was a boarder.

These objective and palpable documents, bearing authentic information, are nevertheless opposed by doubts and questions, which persist throughout the investigation. They are manifested by the many unanswered questions that punctuate the text: "For what reasons did her parents enrol her in this boarding school?" (p. 37); "Was Dora Bruder in the 'ouvroirs' or in the 'classes'?" (p. 39); "Did her parents take Dora to the Ornano 43 cinema [...] or did she go on her own?" (p. 34) Thus, in *Dora Bruder*, Modiano suggests more than he asserts: "She must have played in the Square Clignancourt" (p. 34); "Maybe – but I'm sure of it" (p. 35); "I was reduced to guesswork" (p. 61).

Moreover, the investigation continues beyond the novel and its publication. Modiano appeals to the reader: "In writing this book, I am making appeals, like lighthouse signals which I unfortunately doubt will light up the night. But I still hope." (p. 42). Doubt is always accompanied by hope in the author's search.

Despite the difficulties, Modiano manages to reconstruct Dora's life; he imagines or supposes the missing details: "I can roughly guess the times of day" (p. 39). Yet some unknowns do remain: What happened to Dora during those few weeks of freedom after she ran away? Who did she meet? Where did she go? These questions nag at him: "I'll never know what she spent her days doing, where she hid, who she was with [...]." (p. 144).

THE ROLE OF THE CITY

The fact that the Bruders are modest people makes the investigator's task more difficult: "They are people who leave little trace behind. Almost anonymous. [...] What is known about them often boils down to a simple address. And this topographical precision contrasts with what will forever be unknown about their lives – this blank, this block of unknown and silence." (p. 28).

This is why Modiano relies on tangible elements such as places. The role of the city becomes fundamental in his investigation. He thus explores the streets, the neighbourhood, the school, the hotel room that Dora frequented, because "it is said that at least places keep a slight imprint of the people who inhabited them" (p. 29).

Moreover, Paris, its streets, and the neighbourhood where Dora lived are the only reference shared with the narrator. It is the city that unites them and it is through the city that everything began. When Modiano reads the wanted notice, he has a clear picture of the place where the Bruder family lived; the neighbourhood is familiar to him. Paris is Modiano's only certainty. He knows that Dora lived there, he knows the exact address of her family home, of her school. When he wanders around Paris, he thinks of Dora, he knows that she too has walked these streets.

The emotions, doubts and questions linked to the investigation are underlined by the turbulent aspect of the urban setting, which mirrors the moods of the investigator. The city is presented as a black and white photograph (the black walls of the boarding school, the greyness of Paris, the falling snow): "I had a strange sensation as I walked along the wall of the Lariboisière hospital [...], as if I had entered the darkest part of Paris. But it was simply the contrast between the too-bright lights of the Boulevard de Clichy and the black, endless wall." (p. 29).

In the course of his investigation, Patrick Modiano uncovers places that have been neglected, demolished or razed to the ground over time and brings them back to life. He does the same with Dora, Ernest and the others. Under Patrick Modiano's pen, Paris – and in particular the Clignancourt district – becomes a kind of "place of memory" in the sense of Pierre Nora: "An object becomes a place of memory when it escapes oblivion, for example with the affixing of commemorative plaques, and when a community reinvests it with its affect and emotions." (NORA P. (ed.), *Les lieux de mémoire. La Nation*, tome II, Paris, Gallimard, 1989, p. 7) The city becomes the bearer of Dora Bruder's history, but also of its collective history.

THE DUTY TO REMEMBER

The duty to remember refers to the moral obligation to fight against collective amnesia by maintaining the memory of past suffering experienced by a part of the population. *Dora Bruder* is part of this fight against oblivion, insofar as the work gives an account of the life of the Jews in Paris during the Occupation. Thus, history forms the backdrop of the story. Patrick Modiano tells us about the wearing of the star, the rules imposed on the Jews and those who took sides with them:

- the Jews of France were considered above all as Jews. French nationality did not protect them from deportation. Ernest Bruder is a perfect example, since despite being a French legionnaire, he was deported in the convoy of 18 September 1942 to Auschwitz;

- Modiano recounts the roundups ("From the summer of 42, the area around the Saint-Cœur-de-Marie became particularly dangerous. The roundups followed one another for two years", p. 49), the detention centres, the humiliations, the slow side-lining of part of the population, and the periodic checks Jews experienced ("[…] submit to a 'periodic check' by presenting their identity card", p. 56);

- the Jews had the status of "plague victims" (p. 117), and their families, like the Bruders', were separated and gradually sent to concentration camps. They were obliged to report themselves and all their family members to the authorities, which Dora's father did not do, preferring not to communicate the existence of his daughter;

- from 7 June 1942, Jews had to wear a yellow star. Other rules were added to this, such as the prohibition to leave their homes after eight o'clock in the evening, to cross the "demarcation line" (p. 112) or to own a wireless telegraphy set or a bicycle. Many jobs were still forbidden to Jews who, *de facto*, often lived in poverty, like Dora's mother, who became destitute after her husband was deported;

- some people, considered as "friends of Jews" (p. 141), also voluntarily wore the star in response to the restrictions imposed, sometimes doing so in an eccentric way: "One had tied a star to the neck of her dog. Another had embroidered on it: PAPOU. Another: JENNY. Another had hung eight stars on her belt, each with a letter of VICTORY on it. (p. 140) They will also be arrested."

The author also discusses the role played by French police officers. Indeed, the execution of German orders is entrusted to French policemen, gendarmes and civil servants, "the very ones who are in charge of looking for you and finding you [but who take advantage of this to draw up] files in order to better make you disappear afterwards – definitively." (p. 82). Modiano wonders about their share of responsibility: "At the time of signing, did this civil servant measure the scope of his gesture?" [Moreover, the place to which this young girl was sent was still designated by the Prefecture of Police under a reassuring term: "Hébergement, Centre de séjour surveillé".

Finally, he tells us about the position and experiences of various writers of the time who, like witnesses, also play their role as transmitters of memory by shedding light on this troubled period:

- Felix Hartlaub (German writer, 1913-1945), "died in Berlin in the spring of 1945 [...] in a world of butchery and apocalypse where he found himself by mistake and in a uniform that had been imposed on him, but was not his own' (p. 95);

- Friedo Lampe (German writer, 1899-1945), mistakenly shot by two Russian soldiers at the end of the war (Pp. 93-94).

Thus, in *Dora Bruder*, Patrick Modiano works to revive collective memory by depicting pictures and people who are always very complex and full of ambiguities. In this sense, his work as a novelist is coupled with that of a historian, through which he attempts to give an objective account of reality, without taking sides. In doing so, working for the duty of remembrance, he saves Dora and her family, as well as other unknowns (Claudette Bloch, Josette Delimal, Tamara Isserlis, Hena, etc.) from being forgotten.

AVENUES FOR REFLECTION

SOME IDEAS FOR FURTHER REFLECTION...

- In an interview in April 1997, Patrick Modiano says: "For almost six years, I thought I would never manage to bring Dora Bruder out" ("Dora Bruder, de Patrick Modiano. ("*Dora Bruder*, de Patrick Modiano. Entretien", in *gallimard.fr*, April 1997). In the narrative, he writes: "If I were not there to write it, there would be no trace of the presence of this unknown woman and that of my father in a salad basket in 1942." (p. 65). In light of these statements, explain the importance of writing about the past.

- Modiano explains: "I was so haunted by Dora Bruder that I wrote a novel in 1989 after reading the wanted notice. I didn't know anything yet about what I found today. I wrote this novel, *Voyage de noces*, to try to fill the void I felt when I thought of Dora Bruder, about whom I knew nothing. But when the novel was finished, I was back to the same point. And all this could only end in a book that would not be a novel." (*ibid.*). In your opinion, is Dora Bruder a work of fiction? What kind of work is it?

- Why does Modiano consider that a novel is not enough? Comment on this.

- The author delivers a precise and methodical investigation, but despite everything, a mystery remains:

Where did Dora live during these few weeks of running away? Who did she see? What did she do? Imagine and tell us.

- "I realise that I had to write 200 pages to capture, unconsciously, a vague reflection of reality." (p. 54). Is writing the best instrument against forgetting? Argue and give examples.

- Speaking of the letters addressed to the police prefect during the Occupation, Modiano says: "Today we can read them. Those to whom they were addressed did not want to take them into account, and now it is we, who were not yet born at that time, who are the recipients and the guardians." (p. 84). Comment.

- What relationship does the author have with the city of Paris?

- How is the responsibility of the Vichy regime in the Shoah portrayed in *Dora Bruder*?

- What relationship to literature does the narrator have in the novel?

- Many anonymous people, also victims of the Second World War, are evoked by Modiano. How? What is at stake in this process?

TO GO FURTHER

REFERENCE EDITION

MODIANO P., *Dora Bruder*, Paris, Gallimard, « Folio » collection, 2015.

BENCHMARK STUDIES

BEM J., « Dora Bruder ou la biographie déplacée de Modiano », in *Cahiers de l'Association internationale des études françaises*, volume 52, n° 1, 2000, p. 221-232.

COLONNA V. *L'autofiction, essai sur la fictionalisation de soi en littérature*, Paris, EHESS, 1989.

"*Dora Bruder*, by Patrick Modiano. Interview", in *gallimard.fr*, April 1997, accessed on July 7, 2017, http://www.gallimard.fr/Media/Gallimard/Entretien-ecrit/Entretien-Patrick-Modiano-Dora-Bruder

FERENCZI T. (ed.), *Devoir de mémoire, droit à l'oubli?* Paris, Complexe, 2002.

LEVI P., *Le devoir de mémoire*, Paris, Mille et une nuits, 1995.

MADELÉNAT D., *La biographie*, Paris, Presses universitaires de France, 1984.

NORA P. (dir.), *Les lieux de mémoire. La Nation, tome II*, Paris, Gallimard, 1989.

Although the editor makes every effort to verify the accuracy of the information published, BrightSummaries.com accepts no responsibility for the content of this book.

www.brightsummaries.com

Ebook EAN: 9782808686570
Paperback EAN: 9782808697972
Legal Deposit: D/2023/12603/1077

Cover: © Primento
Digital conception by Primento, the digital partner of publishers.